DISCARD

NATURAL HISTORY FROM A TO Z

A Terrestrial Sampler

ALSO WRITTEN AND ILLUSTRATED BY TIM ARNOLD:
The Winter Mittens

ILLUSTRATED BY TIM ARNOLD:
Worlds I Know by Myra Cohn Livingston
Least of All by Carol Purdy

NATURAL HISTORY FROM A TO Z

A Terrestrial Sampler

written and illustrated
by Tim Arnold

MARGARET K. MCELDERRY BOOKS
NEW YORK

MAXWELL MACMILLAN CANADA
TORONTO
MAXWELL MACMILLAN INTERNATIONAL
NEW YORK • OXFORD • SINGAPORE • SYDNEY

Margaret K. McElderry Books
Macmillan Publishing Company
866 Third Avenue,
New York, NY 10022

Maxwell Macmillan Canada, Inc.
1200 Eglinton Avenue East, Suite 200
Don Mills, Ontario M3C 3N1

Macmillan Publishing Company is part of the
Maxwell Communication Group of Companies.

Printed in Hong Kong
First Edition
10 9 8 7 6 5 4 3 2 1

Library of Congress Cataloging-in-Publication Data
Arnold, Tim.
Natural history from A to Z / Tim Arnold — 1st ed.
p.   cm.
1. Animals — Dictionaries, Juvenile. 1. Title.
QL49.A76 1991   591 — dc19   88—26879 CIP AC
ISBN 0-689-50467-5

for Elise
with thanks to
Jay Evans

Introduction

The word *Terrestrial* in the subtitle of this book refers to the fact that every plant or animal described is (or was) a land or land-based organism.

Sampler refers to the use of the alphabet. In America's colonial days, needlework samplers often used the alphabet as a way to demonstrate a beginner's skill in embroidering a variety of stitches. This book introduces the reader to a variety of plants, animals, and *ideas* in the broad field of natural history, which I hope may inspire further reading and study.

Tim Arnold

A
Anteaters (and Aardvarks)

Anteaters belong to the most primitive of the New World animal families, the Edentates, which includes the sloths, the armadillos, and the anteaters. There are three distinct species of anteaters, all having similar forms. The giant anteater is perhaps the most striking of the three.

silky anteater   *giant anteater*   *tamandua*

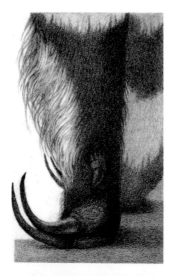

It is the size of a large dog and is covered with stiff hair that is short at the head, long and bushy at the tail, and somewhere in between on the body. It is terrestrial, spending most of its time on the ground, whereas its smaller cousins are likely to spend some of their time in the trees.

This slow-moving mammal's diet consists almost entirely of ants and termites. The powerful front legs with their sharp claws can break open an anthill or termite nest with a single blow and are an effective defense against their chief predators, jaguars and pumas. The long snout pushes down through the loose dirt so that the anteater's tongue can reach the center of the nest. It can push this long, sticky tongue in and out of its mouth up to 160 times per minute—which requires an unusually large number of salivary glands to keep the tongue moist.

The insects are swallowed whole and ground up in the muscular stomach, which has a rough lining for just that purpose. As a result, the giant anteater has long since lost the teeth it originally had in the distant past. Its appearance may be ungainly, but it is perfectly adapted for this way of life. A giant anteater can consume some 25,000 to 30,000 ants and termites in a day.

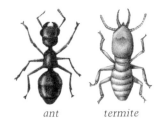
ant   *termite*

In the eighteenth century the anteater and the aardvark of Africa were mistakenly classified together. It is easy to see why. The aardvark feeds primarily on termites and occasionally on ants. It, too, has a long, tubular snout and a sticky tongue to collect its meals. It, too, has powerful, clawed front legs that tear open nests and dig burrows.

Above: The aardvark uses its sensitive ears to hear insects.

Despite those similarities, there are many physical differences between the two that lead to the conclusion that they are not closely related. The process at work here is known as convergent evolution, in which two (or more) unrelated animals may develop strikingly similar features for accomplishing a task — in this case, making a living at efficiently consuming termites and ants.

B

Basenji

The basenji, also known as the barkless dog, is one of the oldest dog breeds. Basenji types appear in Egyptian tomb paintings from as long ago as 2700 B.C. Basenjis are known to have been gifts to the pharaohs and, along with the five other distinct breeds kept by the Egyptians, to have held a place of honor in that society.

Basenjis are relatively small dogs, measuring about 17 inches at the shoulders as adults. Their glossy coat is short and sheds very little. It is a chestnut red or fawn color with white markings, usually on the feet, chest, or curled tail. The features are sharp and inquisitive-looking, the ears firm and pointed. Basenjis are clean, washing themselves in a catlike fashion. They are intelligent, loyal and eager to please, good with children, and, as has been mentioned, have no bark.

Above: Egyptian dog breeds based on tomb paintings

Some basenjis are black and white, as shown here.

The bark has probably been lacking since the early days of the breed, when basenjis were used as hunting dogs in northern Africa. In addition to being brave and possessing a keen scent, the dog was silent, which surely made it an effective hunter of small game.

The Egyptians domesticated, or tried to domesticate, a variety of other animals for hunting, including the leopard, the cheetah, and even the lion. Domestication is the bringing of a previously wild animal into close association with humans. It might be guessed that efforts to domesticate the wild cats met with limited success. Yet dogs were, and still are, highly trainable, reliable animals that occupy a place close to our hearts and homes. How did that come to be so?

Since the answer lies before the beginnings of written history, scientists and dog enthusiasts can only make educated guesses. Dogs were probably the first domesticated animals, and the process was probably slow and at first unintentional. One theory suggests that a few ancient wolves might have discovered that they could eat well on discarded meat and animal remains if they followed men on the hunt. A tentative bond might have formed that way and, after many years, developed into a hunting partnership. The wolves' keen scent and stealth would have been useful in thick forest, just as the basenjis' was only a few thousand years ago.

In the time since the bond was formed, domesticated dogs have been bred and trained as hunters, guards, shepherds, soldiers, beasts of burden, and seekers of the lost. They have been glorified and worshipped, as well as villified and used in cruel, bloody sport. Though they still perform many practical tasks, domesticated dogs like the basenji have become, first and foremost, good friends and companions.

5

C

Coatimundi

The coatimundi, or coati, is a member of the family Procyanidae, which also includes the raccoons and ringtails. It is a little smaller than the raccoon and can be found from southern Arizona to Argentina. The name "coatimundi" originally referred to the adult male of the species, but is now interchangeable with "coati."

coatimundi   *raccoon*   *ringtail*

These mammals have reddish brown to black fur on the back and sides, with yellowish to brown on the undersides. The feet are black, and the chin and throat are whitish. The snout is flexible and mobile and is useful in rooting for food. The banded tail is sometimes used for balance in climbing.

Coatis are diurnal. That is, they hunt, groom, and rest during the day and take to the trees at night to sleep. They prefer fruit when it is available, but also forage for insects. Males will eat large rodents in addition to insects and spiders when the local fruit supply is low.

Coatis generally travel in small groups, made up of females and immature males, though in some populations the groups may consist of as many as twenty individuals. Males more than two years old are kept away from such groups by the combined efforts of the females and sometimes the young except during the breeding season, when one adult male is allowed into the group. That male is permitted to mate with the females, and he defends that position against other males.

There are good reasons for this unusual arrangement. Because the adult males become carnivorous when fruit supplies are low, they must be kept away lest in their hunger they prey on the young coatis. It is for this reason, as well, that the breeding season coincides with the greatest abundance of fruit. Not only do the newborn coatis get plenty to eat, but they can be more safely raised because the adult males also get plenty of fruit and thus present less of a threat.

From left: Wildebeests, lions, and fur seals are all social animals.

Animals that, like coatimundis, live in groups are known as social animals. Social behavior is common in the natural world and provides many benefits. For instance, many animals find it more effective to forage in groups than singly, spreading out to cover more ground and sharing large food supplies when they are found. Prey animals, those that are hunted and eaten by others, may find security in numbers, whereas predators may use group hunting to stalk and kill their prey more efficiently. Social animals can find warmth in cold weather by huddling together or may benefit from the availability of mates in a large group. As the coatis' social structure suggests, the nature of their habitat strongly influences the way the animals behave together.

D
Dragonfly

Roughly 75 percent of all land animals are either birds or insects. The one characteristic that has made such success possible is the ability to fly. And if you have ever been near a lake or pond in summer, you know that the dragonfly is among the most accomplished aeronauts of all.

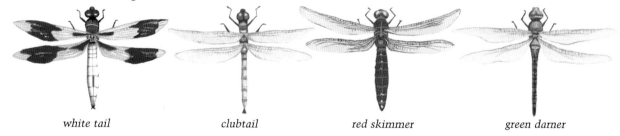

white tail   *clubtail*   *red skimmer*   *green darner*

It is also one of the oldest flying insects, with fossils placing its beginnings at 230 million to 280 million years ago. It was, and still is, primarily tropical; only 412 of the 4,500 species live in our temperate North America.

These ancient fliers are predators, using their incredible mobility to catch the insects they eat in flight, aided by large compound eyes, which give them a wide field of vision. The legs are held in basket fashion to capture the prey but are otherwise weak and used only for perching. Dragonflies have a long, thin abdomen that is well suited for flight, and two sets of wings, which can move independently of one another. The insects' graceful hovering and darting maneuvers make us wish we could take to the air and follow.

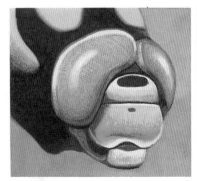

From left: Close-ups of a dragonfly's large eyes, wings in motion, and a wing tip

Some basic principles of aerodynamics (the mechanics of flight) show why an unaided man can't get off the ground and a dragonfly can. The first thing needed for flight is a steady upward force to overcome the pull of gravity. A helium balloon rises because its *total* weight is less than that of the air around it. The air displaced by the balloon forces it upward, much as a hollow, air-filled ball released under water will pop to the surface.

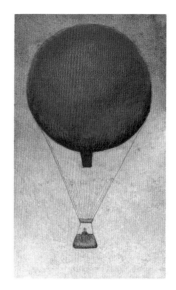

A man is clearly too heavy to rise this way, but so is the dragonfly, even though it is much lighter. It gains this upward force by flapping its broad wings at high speeds, forcing air down. Of course, the dragonfly does not simply rise like a balloon. It moves forward as well as upward. By twisting its wings on each stroke, the dragonfly pushes air both down and back and is propelled forward as it rises. A man, with thin arms instead of wings, cannot displace nearly enough air to overcome his weight and must watch from the ground.

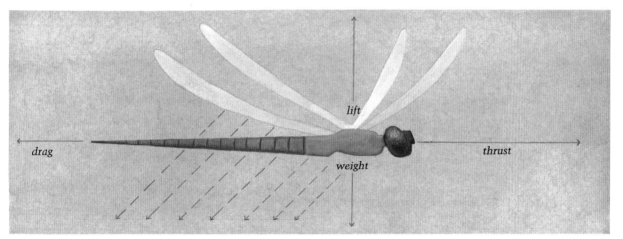

In order for any object to maintain a level flight, its thrust (forward motion) and its lift (upward motion) must balance its drag (wind resistance) and its weight (downward pull of gravity). The dragonfly's more amazing maneuvers, such as hovering, sudden changes of direction, and even flying backward, involve complicated aerodynamic principles. The study of the dragonfly's movements has already helped us improve the maneuverability of our own flying machines.

E

Eohippus

Sixty million years ago, at the dawn of the most recent geological era (the Eocene), lived a small, active, browsing animal named Eohippus. Eohippus was from 10 to 20 inches tall at the shoulder. It had a long, thick tail; three working toes on the front feet, four on the back; and teeth suitable for biting and grinding leaves. It lived in what is now North America, in the tropical and semitropical climates of the time.

Above: Skull of a hyrax

Below: A young Charles Darwin

The first fossil remains of Eohippus were found in England in the 1830s and were given the name Hyracotherium, because of their resemblance to the modern-day hyrax, a small mammal. It was widely believed in those days that all species of plants and animals were "immutable"—that is, that they had been created as we see them and were not subject to change. Fossil animals like *Hyracotherium* were thought to be seperate species that had simply become extinct. A number of people disagreed, however, maintaining that animals and plants change over many years, developing from different, older species.

Charles Darwin, with the publication of *The Origin of Species* in 1859, was the first to support the idea of gradual change with massive amounts of evidence, much of which he collected on his travels around the world. His theory of "descent with modification" soon won wide acceptance among scientists.

Darwin argued that a number of factors, including competition for food and resources, the physical nature of the habitat, and inheritance (or heredity), cause gradual changes in the forms and behavior of plants and animals from generation to generation over long periods of time. He predicted that fossil finds would reveal those changes. Soon the race was on to find such fossils.

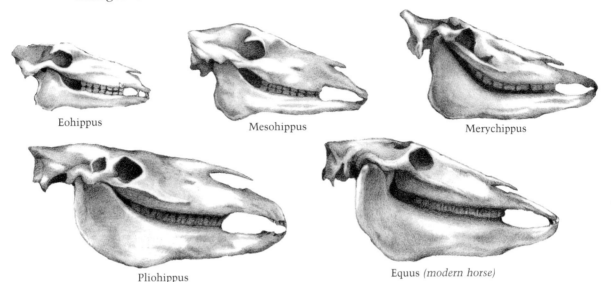

Eohippus

Mesohippus

Merychippus

Pliohippus

Equus *(modern horse)*

Among the most convincing was a series of horse skeletons found mostly in the United States. The skeletons showed a definite chronological sequence and unmistakable changes in size, shape, and skeletal structure. In the latter part of the nineteenth century, it was determined that little *Hyracotherium*, far from being an extinct sort of hyrax, was the earliest known member of the horse family. It was then given the name Eohippus, or "Dawn Horse," though *Hyracotherium* remains its scientific name.

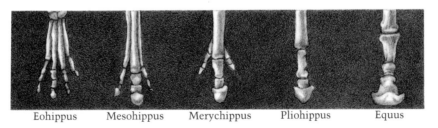

Eohippus   Mesohippus   Merychippus   Pliohippus   Equus

In the more than one hundred years since Darwin's day, a great deal of knowledge has been collected on this subject, now broadly known as evolution. Darwin's notion of the gradual change of species has been greatly expanded, added to, and in some respects corrected. Nevertheless, his ideas remain at the heart of this field of study.

F

Fern

Ferns belong to the group that accounts for the fewest species in the plant kingdom. The Pteridophytes, as they are called, consist of about 10,000 species of ferns and related plants. Many of the original members of the group have become extinct, including some tree ferns that grew to tremendous heights in ancient forests and jungles. Most of the ferns we see today developed in the last 100 million years. That is a long time ago when compared to the history of the human race, but a short time when compared to the 3 billion years since the emergence of the first simple plant cells.

Ferns are found in all but the most inhospitable parts of the world. This wide range has been made possible by the ferns' reproductive method, in which huge numbers of tiny, light spores are released from cases at the proper time of year and carried away by the wind. Some of the spores stay in the air for years and manage to travel long distances. If they happen to land in a moist place, the growth of a new fern starts soon after.

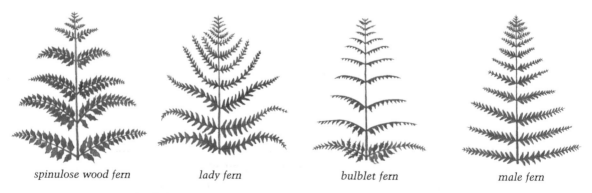

spinulose wood fern   lady fern   bulblet fern   male fern

Ferns lack both seeds and flowers but have in common with trees and flowering plants the vascular tissue that enables them to have firm forms and to transport water and nutrients to all their parts.

The leaves of the ostrich fern grow in a way typical of true ferns, starting with a tightly coiled "fiddlehead" that unfurls to reveal the leaves and leaflets. The ostrich fern is common in North America. It thrives, as many ferns do, along riverbanks and streams or near lakes, ponds, and marshy areas. The stem divides the handsome fronds down the middle, and the veins divide the leaves and their individual leaflets.

From left: The frond, leaf, and leaflets of an ostrich fern

A plant, animal, or object made this way is said to possess symmetry. In the case of the ostrich fern, the symmetry is referred to as bilateral. This means that if an imaginery line is drawn down the center of a form, the sides to the left and right of this axis are the same. Thus, the fronds, leaves, and leaflets of the ostrich fern are all bilaterally symmetrical.

Above: A housefront and a Roman design display bilateral symmetry

Above: A Chinese design and a snowflake display radial symmetry.

Radial symmetry refers to sameness around a central point or axis. A circle and a sphere are both radially symmetrical, as are snowflakes and many flowers. Symmetry in nature has long been studied and admired. Regular patterns and structures emphasize the sense of order found in the shapes and forms of our world. Symmetry can be found applied in many human disciplines, from art and architecture to engineering and mathematics. You need never look far to find an example of it.

G

Galápagos Tortoise

Tortoises are those members of the turtle family that live primarily on land. Like other turtles, they have hard shells into which they can retreat, they lay eggs, which they do not incubate, and they have beaklike jaws that shear off chunks of food. They have small but well-developed brains and rely particularly on the senses of smell and sight. Tortoises range in size from very large to very small.

Aldabra Island tortoise *radiated tortoise* *Berlandier's tortoise* *gopher tortoise* *desert tortoise*

One of the largest is the Galápagos tortoise, a species found exclusively on the Galápagos Islands. This giant tortoise reaches a size of up to 5 feet long and 2½ feet high, and a weight approaching 500 pounds. It has been known to live well beyond one hundred years. It has regular living habits, walking each day on well-worn paths to drink, wallow in water, and feed on nearby plants. It spends its nights in regularly used sleeping areas.

At one time the tortoises were abundant on all of the Galápagos Islands. Unfortunately, they were easy prey for whalers, pirates, and other seafarers stopping to replenish their meat supplies. Later rats and pigs gone wild, first introduced by European colonists, further lessened the tortoises' numbers by feeding on their eggs. Now the giant reptiles are found on only seven of the fifteen islands.

Charles Darwin visited the Galápagos archipelago in the mid-nineteenth century, when the tortoises were still plentiful. He was struck by the fact that each island had a somewhat different type of tortoise. He also noticed differences from island to island in certain species of birds, lizards, and insects. Those observations provided support for Darwin's notion that species change over the years. The geographical separation and slightly different environment of each island worked to produce animals that were different from one another yet clearly closely related.

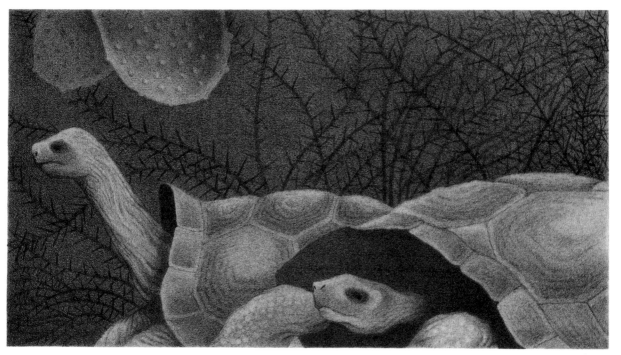

These two varieties of the Galápagos tortoise show the kinds of changes Darwin observed. One has developed a notch in its shell, which allows it to stretch up and feed on juicy cactus.

That process of separation and change is called speciation. Speciation is a slow process in which members of a species—that is, a population of like animals that cannot or do not breed successfully with members of another—become separated from their fellows and, over many generations, influenced by their environment, change enough so that they can no longer breed with the original population. They have become a distinct species.

Since the process is too slow to be observed in a single lifetime, Darwin looked not only for closely related (but different) species, but for animal populations on their way to becoming distinct species. The Galápagos tortoise may well be such an animal—markedly different from island to island but still belonging to a single species.

H

Honeybee

Honeybees are social creatures that, unlike coatis (see *C*), *always* belong to well-organized groups numbering in the tens of thousands. The groups are so well organized that they give the appearance of acting with a single mind. Although individual bees die, the hive continues year after year, through winter cold and summer heat.

Three kinds of adult bees can be found in a honeybee hive. The queen bee has a long, slender abdomen that distinguishes her from the other females. She is responsible for all of the egg laying in the hive and can lay hundreds a day throughout her life. Male bees, or drones, are roundish in shape and small brained. Only a small number of the hundreds of drones in a hive will mate with the queen or with a young queen leaving to start a new hive. The drones serve no other purpose and are forced out of the hive or killed after the mating season. Queens have only one mating flight in their three- to four-year lives.

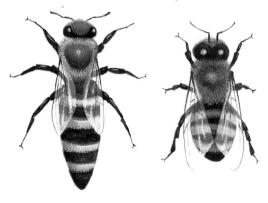

queen   *drone*   *A comb under construction, bustling with activity*

The third type of honeybee is the one that makes the hive function. This is the worker bee. Workers are non-egg-laying females that perform a number of important jobs, in a sequence that each bee follows as it matures. In the first stage of their lives, young workers clean empty cells in the comb so that eggs can be laid in them. Later they feed the larvae, or developing bees, which stay in the cells until they reach maturity. In the second stage of life the worker bees perform one or more "indoor" jobs. They may store nectar in food cells, they may clean debris and dead bees from the hive, or they may act as sentries protecting the hive against all intruders.

The final stage of the worker bees' life is the one we are most familiar with. The bees become foragers, flying out to collect pollen and nectar from flowers and bringing it back to the hive.

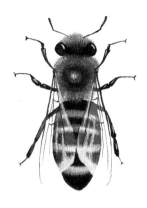

Above: A worker bee
Below: Workers foraging

One of the most fascinating aspects of honeybee society is its system of communication. The bees communicate by means of a dance and scent language first observed and described by Karl von Frisch. Workers returning from foraging flights perform tail-wiggling dances that communicate accurately the location of the flowers they have found. The scent of the flowers is also detected by the other workers, which can then fly to that place in large numbers.

A typical honey bee "dance" with tail wiggling

Although the social structure of the honeybees is much more intricate and efficient than the coatis', the benefits are basically the same. The hive life provides warmth, protection, a shared food supply, and a better life than the individual bee could manage on its own. It is not surprising, then, that people have long admired these industrious little insects.

I

Ivy

The familiar ivy plant is found in the wild as well as in the garden, in the home, and on buildings. It is an evergreen, keeping its leaves year round. Deciduous plants and trees shed theirs each autumn. This hardy plant is often described as a "climber" because it has the ability to do just that, with the aid of rootlike "stem suckers," which allow it to cling fast to many kinds of surfaces. Mature ivies can be identified by the flowers and berries they produce. Some plants take many years to reach that stage.

Heron   *Goldheart*   *Sulfur Heart*   Canariensis   *Adam*   Deltoidea

Ivy is a highly adaptable plant. It grows well in a variety of climates and soils. For that reason, it is valued by gardeners and has been cultivated for hundreds of years. As a garden plant it comes in many shapes, sizes, and shades. It is attractive growing on the sides of buildings and is often seen there, but is also commonly used on fences, on trellises, and as ground cover. As ground cover, it helps prevent soil erosion and chokes out weeds. On any surface its canopy of leaves provides a haven for insects, nesting birds, and other creatures.

The plant's ability to climb gives it an advantage many other plants don't have—mobility. A tree or shrub is rooted to a spot and can grow only a certain distance up and out. The growth of ivy is limited only by the size and shape of the host and the life span of the ivy itself. On a large building, over the years a single plant can spread a considerable distance in all directions.

Like all green plants, ivies feed themselves by the process we call photosynthesis. In photosynthesis carbon dioxide from the air and water from the soil are converted into carbohydrates (natural sugars), which sustain the plant. A very valuable by-product of this process is oxygen, which the plant releases into the atmosphere and which in turn helps to sustain all animal life.

Photosynthesis cannot take place in the dark. Light, usually sunlight, allows the process to occur. Light is the "catalyst" that helps the plant convert low-energy ingredients into high-energy food. Small wonder that plants work so hard to maximize the amount of sun they receive.

Ivies thriving on host trees

Ivy, by virtue of its mobility, is particularly good at moving to advantageous, sunny spots. It simply climbs until some part of the plant is receiving sufficient light. In fact, if it is left unpruned, ivy sometimes grows so well that the burden of its weight on a host tree causes both plants to be uprooted and overturned by high winds.

J
Jaguar

The jaguar is one of the big cats, a group that includes the leopard, the snow leopard, the lion, and the tiger. It is primarily a jungle animal, whose largest populations are in the tropical Amazon basin of South America. Its range extends, however, as far north as Mexico and as far south as Argentina, where it can be found in such diverse habitats as grassland, desert, and low mountains.

Jaguars are imposing cats, though they are smaller than either the lion or the tiger. Their well-muscled, compact bodies and sharp teeth and claws leave no doubt about their carnivorous nature. Adult males reach lengths of about 6 feet (plus tail) and weights of 250 pounds and more. Females are somewhat smaller. Their coats are short and pale yellow to tawny, overlaid with striking rosettes of black or dark brown. Black jaguars are fairly common.

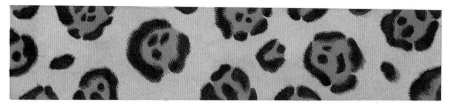

These big cats maintain territories, which they mark off with their urine. In areas where the population is dense and competition for food is keen, territories are strictly observed. Jaguars are not social animals. They are loners except during the mating season, when they pair up briefly and may form temporary, small groups.

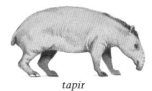

capybara   *peccary*   *tapir*

They prey on both large and small animals, including deer, capybaras, peccaries, tapirs, lizards, snakes, and birds. After making a kill and eating its fill, the cat's powerful jaws and limbs allow it to drag the carcass, sometimes a long way, to a spot where it is hidden for later feeding.

The jaguars' success as hunters is due in part to their markings. The pattern of light and dark on their coats looks very like the play of light and shadow on dense jungle foliage. That makes the jaguars difficult to see as they lie in wait or stalk their prey. Such markings are known as camouflage. Camouflage helps predators like the jaguars to conceal themselves, and it also helps prey animals to conceal themselves from predators. It even assists some animals that are both hunter and hunted.

From left: The snowshoe hare, the bittern, and the Malaysian tree frog employ camouflage for protection.

Unfortunately, the beauty of the jaguar's coat has contributed to its sharply reduced numbers. Some people feel compelled to wear the coat on themselves, and so a great many cats have been killed for their pelts. Jaguars have also been hunted because they are a source of meat and because they are feared. In addition, expanding human populations have reduced jaguar territories. As a result, the jaguars have been listed by a number of conservancy groups as threatened or endangered.

K

Kiwi

The ratites are a well-known group of flightless birds, of which the kiwi, native to New Zealand, is a member. The rhea, the emu, the cassowary, and the ostrich are also ratites. All of these birds have vestigal wings; that is, wings that have become small and useless. These, along with skeletal and muscular features, indicate that the ratites did fly at some time in the distant past.

cassowary   rhea   ostrich   emu

The kiwi is perhaps the most unusual of this unusual group of birds. Its head and eyes are small, and it uses its long, thin beak to probe among rocks and in dirt for food. The kiwi's legs are thick and strong, and have four sharp-clawed toes to the foot. The feathers are brown to gray-brown and almost hairy in appearance.

Above: A giant moa and a kiwi

Kiwis are secretive, solitary animals. They come out at night to feed on insects, larvae, berries, and worms. Calls of "kee-wee" can be heard as they forage. During the day they stay well hidden in small caves or holes in the ground. They prefer wooded areas but can be found fairly high up in the mountains, too.

At one time New Zealand was the home of many species of flightless birds. One of them, the giant moa, reached a maximum size of 13 feet tall and 500 pounds in weight. Fossil evidence suggests that moas had been around for at least a million years, possibly 2 million. Only three hundred years ago they disappeared completely, hunted out of existence by the islands' human inhabitants.

When a species of animals no longer exists, it is said to be extinct. Very simply, it is gone and will never again be seen on earth. Extinctions are a natural part of the cycles of life. They have always occurred. Sometimes they are the result of a massive natural catastrophe, such as a prolonged drought or a sudden climatic change. Or they may occur when one species cannot compete successfully with another for food in a given area.

From left: The Galápagos land iguana, the scimitar-horned oryx, and the ocelot. All are threatened with extinction.

From left: The numbat, the kit fox, and the prairie chicken are also endangered.

Unfortunately, extinctions have frequently occurred as a result of human actions. The moa's disappearance is only one of many, many examples. Excessive hunting, expanding human populations, and pollution have caused extinctions around the world. Many of them need not have happened. Many can be prevented. It was feared, for example, that the kiwi might go the way of the giant moa, but the little bird has been strictly protected in New Zealand and is now doing very well.

L

Ladybug

The ladybug is a small, unobtrusive insect that is a member of the Coleoptera, the beetles. It is also known as the ladybird, the ladybeetle, and the ladybug beetle. The beetles are far and away the largest group of insects, with 300,000 species around the world, 4,000 of which are varieties of the ladybug.

Japanese beetle   *darkling beetle*   *stag beetle*   *soldier beetle*   *June bug*   *wood-boring beetle*

Ladybugs, and all beetles, are protected by their hard forewings. When the forewings are folded against their bodies, they act as armor. In flight they open and allow the thinner, membranous hind wings to do most of the work. Ladybugs are not great aerialists, nor do they need to be. They spend most of their time on the ground or in foliage. They do not feed while flying, as dragonflies do (see *D*), and when threatened or startled they are as likely to let go of their perch and drop to the ground like a stone as to fly away. When they do fly, ladybugs must climb to an elevated spot to catch the breeze. They then open their protective wings and take off. Perhaps you have seen one do this from the tip of your finger.

  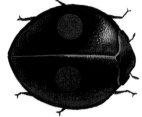

lateral ladybug   *California ladybug*   *twice-stabbed ladybug*

Those species of ladybugs with the familiar red-orange to orange color enjoy protection from some predators, particularly birds. Many insects with this coloration are for some reason bad tasting. Birds that have tasted them once learn pretty quickly to avoid them thereafter. The effectiveness of this defense is one reason ladybugs seem rather fearless and are easily caught and examined by curious humans.

It is sometimes said that the number of spots on a ladybug's shell indicates how many years old it is. That is not so. The number of spots usually depends on the species of ladybug. There are, for instance, the two-spotted ladybug, the six-spotted ladybug, and the eighteen-spotted ladybug.

On one species, called the convergent ladybug, the number of spots on the shell differs from bug to bug. Some have many, some none at all. Differences, such as these and less obvious ones, between members of the same species are called variations. Individual variations are inevitable because all young are born with a mixture of characteristics inherited from both parents. The offspring may resemble one parent more than the other but will *never* be an exact copy of either. Even ladybugs with exactly the same number of spots differ from one another.

These three brothers look very much like each other but have distinct differences.

We recognize individual variation easily where people are concerned. Shape, size, coloring, and facial features distinguish one person from another. Differences between members of other animal species may be less apparent to us, especially in small ones like the ladybug. They are there, however, if we look carefully. Every individual is unique.

M

Mammallike Reptiles

The mammallike reptiles, or Therapsidae, were found on all the continents some 200 million years ago. They have been so named because they were reptiles with anatomical resemblances to the primitive mammals that arose millions of years later. Along with large amphibians and primitive reptiles, the mammallike reptiles were the dominant animals of their day. There were three distinct types.

Lystrosaurus, a dicynodont

Moschops, a dinocephalian

The dicynodonts were the most numerous and widespread. They were medium-sized plant eaters that were able to compete successfully with other reptiles and endure for millions of years.

The dinocephalians were the largest of the therapsids and among the largest creatures of their age, though they were considerably smaller than the giant dinosaurs that succeeded them. Some of the dinocephalians were plant eaters, and some were meat eaters.

Thrinaxadon, a theriodont

The theriodonts were the most important of the three types because it was from this group that the first true mammals eventually developed. The theriodonts had what are now considered mammalian characteristics. Their legs, for example, were longer than those of other reptiles and closer to the central axis of the body. That enabled them to run with more speed and agility and, most likely, to hunt more efficiently than their competitors.

Their teeth were "differentiated," as many mammals' today are, with cutting incisors, sharp, tearing canines, and flat, chopping cheek teeth. These allowed for quicker eating and digestion and, therefore, quicker absorption of nutrients, which in turn allowed the theriodonts to be even more active in their hunting.

By about 180 million years ago, the mammallike reptiles had died out. They were succeeded by new groups of reptiles, including the turtles, the crocodilians, and the dinosaurs. These would dominate the earth for 110 million years, during which time some of the most remarkable and impressive creatures ever to live evolved.

In the past two hundred years, the study of the structure of the earth and of the fossils found in it has revealed that the story of life is much longer and more complicated than had previously been thought. In order to describe, in a general way, the changes that have taken place over these hundreds of millions of years, geological time, as it is referred to, is divided into the following eras and periods, each marking a major change or event.

ERA	PERIOD	DURATION IN YEARS	BEGAN HOW MANY YEARS AGO!	SOME IMPORTANT CHANGES
Cenozoic	Quaternary	2,500,000	2,500,000	Homo sapiens (man) ice age
	Tertiary	62,500,000	65,000,000	early hominids spread of mammals
Mesozoic	Cretaceous	70,000,000	135,000,000	extinction of dinosaurs
	Jurassic	55,000,000	190,000,000	first birds
	Triassic	35,000,000	225,000,000	dinosaurs, early mammals
Paleozoic	Permian	55,000,000	280,000,000	mammallike reptiles
	Carboniferous	65,000,000	345,000,000	first reptiles
	Devonian	50,000,000	395,000,000	fishes, amphibians
	Silurian	35,000,000	430,000,000	airbreathing animals
	Ordovician	70,000,000	500,000,000	vertebrates
	Cambrian	70,000,000	570,000,000	marine invertebrates
Precambrian		4,030,000,000	4,600,000,000	primitive marine animals

It is important to bear in mind the *huge* amounts of time these divisions represent. Only over so many millions of years could the changes in the shapes and sizes and sorts of creatures on the earth have taken place.

N

Neanderthal Man

In 1856 the partial skeleton of a primitive hominid was unearthed in the Neander Valley near Düsseldorf, Germany. Similar types were found in Belgium in the 1880s, elsewhere in Europe, and around the world after the turn of the twentieth century. Neanderthal man, as it soon became known, was, after much study and debate, accepted as a predecessor of modern man and as having lived before and during the last ice age.

Neanderthal skulls and a re-creation of a Neanderthal man

Neanderthals walked fully erect and were from 5 to 5½ feet tall. They were compact of body and limb and well muscled. They had pronounced ridges over the eyes and a somewhat flattened skull shape. Their brain size was similar to that of modern man. Neanderthals tended to have receding chins, broad, flattened noses, and massive jaws, though there seems to have been a fair amount of individual variation.

These early humans lived in a variety of climates and habitats, ranging from subtropical to coastal to the harsh conditions of ice-age Europe. It is the latter we are most familiar with, through popular literature and movies. We admire the toughness and ingenuity that must have been necessary for survival. Ice-age Neanderthals often lived in caves and sometimes built additional wood shelters inside them. They were proficient hunters, preying primarily on the abundant reindeer that grazed on the tundra and also on more difficult prey, such as the bison and woolly mammoth.

Neanderthals made a variety of stone tools with which to hunt, butcher animals, and work skins for clothing. They used flint-chipping techniques that had been passed on for tens of thousands of years. Neanderthals were not grunting brutes. They probably possessed a complex language and society, with rituals to improve the success of hunting and with burials that suggest a belief in an afterlife.

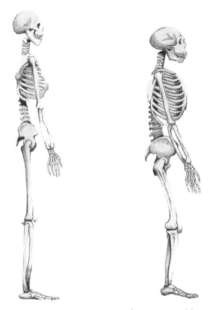

Skeleton of a modern man (Homo sapiens) *next to a Neanderthal skeleton*

Before the last ice age ended, Neanderthals disappeared from the earth. What became of them is still a matter for debate. Some interpretations of the fossil evidence suggest that during this time a portion of the Neanderthal culture evolved into a more sophisticated tool-making society called the Cro-Magnon, a direct ancestor of modern man. Others suggest that the Cro-Magnons migrated to Europe from the east, from Asia, and were able to displace the less organized and developed society of the Neanderthals. This theory holds that Cro-Magnon and Neanderthal man arose from a common ancestor, but that Neanderthal was a "cousin" that became extinct. Whether cousin or direct predessor, Neanderthal was in every way human and an important contributor to the story of human evolution.

O

Orangutan

Orangutans, along with chimpanzees and gorillas, are members of the great apes. Today orangs can be found in jungle forests on the islands of Borneo and Sumatra, though fossil evidence shows that they were at one time widespread in Southeast Asia and parts of China. The rising of the ocean's level many thousands of years ago sealed off what had once been a land bridge to Asia. That isolated some orangutan populations in their present habitats. The mainland populations eventually became extinct.

chimpanzee   *gorilla*

Below: orangutan

Today's orangutans, though smaller than their ancestors, are large primates — sometimes larger and frequently stronger than humans. Their arms are long and powerful, and their hands are suited for grasping tree branches. Both characteristics are typical of tree-dwelling, or arboreal, primates. Orangutans have coarse, reddish orange to reddish brown hair. Adults have fleshy cheek pads, which are particularly prominent on the males.

Orangutans move slowly from branch to branch and tree to tree as they forage for fruit. Their bulk does not allow them to swing with the daring and agility of the gibbons or monkeys. Sometimes they even come to the ground to forage. Their good memories allow them to know exactly which fruit trees are in season and when, so that they can feed accordingly. At night orangs sleep high above the forest floor in platform nests that they build. A fair number have falls at some point in their lives, but orangs have bones that heal remarkably quickly when broken.

These primates, unlike the chimps and gorillas, are not generally social. They pair up during the mating season and to some extent during the raising of the young. In some areas orangs have formed loose groups of ten or so, but this does not seem to be the norm.

A female orangutan and her young in a platform shelter

Orangutan intelligence is thought to be high, but it has been more difficult to observe and test than that of the other apes. The orangutan is called "old man of the forest," and it is easy to see why. The orang's general size and shape and particularly its round, hairless face, fringed with wispy, beardlike hair, can give a remarkably human impression.

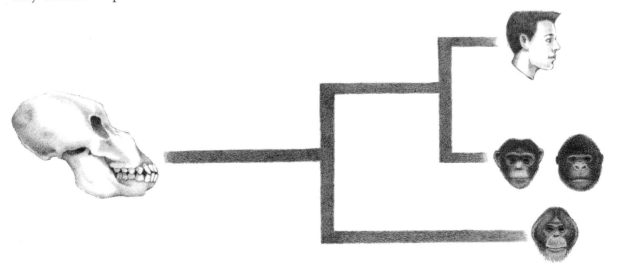

A simple representation of the relationship between humans, chimpanzees, gorillas, orangutans, and a likely common ancestor, proconsul

Indeed, the great apes *are* our closest relatives in the animal world. They may seem like very distant relatives when we consider the complexities and achievements of human society versus the simple jungle life of the apes. But if you compare a human being to a mackerel or a lobster or a termite, the many similarities between human beings and apes become apparent. Both arose from a common ancestor and followed different paths of development and change over a period of some 8 to 15 million years, leading to the present.

P

Penguin

The fourteen living species of penguins are not, as is sometimes thought, found only in Antarctica. They can also be found in the southern parts of New Zealand, Australia, Africa, and South America, and as far north as the equatorial Galápagos Islands. Although penguin species vary in location, size, and weight, they are in most ways very similar.

little blue   *chinstrap*   *king*   *emperor*   *adelie*   *rockhopper*

Like the ratites (see *K*), penguins lost the use of their wings for flight at some point in the distant past. Unlike the kiwi's wings, though, the penguin's did not become useless. They became powerful paddles to propel these aquatic birds through the water, while the feet and tail act as rudders. The sleek, streamlined body is ideal for fancy maneuvering on dives for crustaceans, squid, or fish.

Penguins "porpoising" or diving out of the water as they swim

On land penguins are not so graceful. Because their legs are located at the end of the body, rather than at the middle, they have an upright stance that is both amusing and endearing to human admirers. Despite such awkwardness, penguins seem to prefer the land to the water when threatened. That is because such predators as the leopard seal and the killer whale live in the sea.

The most important land activities for penguins are breeding and raising the young. In most species males and females have lasting "marriages," some enduring for many years and some for only one or two. Males and females generally share the duties of incubating the eggs and then feeding the young once they have hatched. New chicks need plenty of food and care until they grow the waterproof feathers that allow them to dive for themselves.

Male king penguins incubating eggs under a fold of fat

A young king penguin

The greatest numbers of penguins are found in and around Antarctica. To survive in that harsh and frigid part of the world, they have developed a number of ways to keep warm. Their bodies are protected by a layer of blubber and by three dense layers of feathers. An efficient circulatory system also helps conserve body heat. In the water penguins are constantly in motion to help maintain body temperature. On land, during the cold Antarctic winter, huge groups of penguins huddle together for warmth.

Such favorable changes in the body or behavior of an animal in response to the conditions of its environment are called adaptations. Adaptations often occur as a result of more than one aspect of the animal's habitat. Such is the case with the penguin, which has adapted very nicely to the cold Antarctic as well as to life in and near the ocean.

33

Quail

Species of quail can be found in nearly every part of the world. This adaptable bird inhabits such diverse environments as desert, grassland, mountain forest, and jungle. It is a smaller relative of the grouse, ranging in size from 14½ to 3½ inches long.

bobwhite quail   *scaled quail*   *mountain quail*   *harlequin quail*

The quail is particularly widespread in North and Central America, where it has been carefully studied in the wild and raised domestically. It is a plain-looking bird at first glance but actually has beautiful and distinctive patterns in its feathers. Those patterns vary from species to species, and within species they vary depending on the age and sex of the bird. Quail stay within broad home ranges and do not migrate as the seasons change.

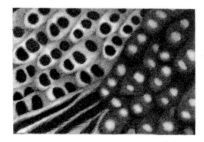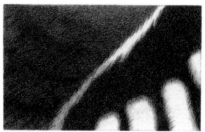

From left: Feather patterns of the harlequin, mountain, and scaled quail

They are social birds, coming together in groups known as coveys, and possess a variety of vocal signals. The size of the covey depends on the species and on the population in a given area. These groups do not have strong hierarchical structures, that is, ones in which individuals have specific roles or status in the group (see *H*). Coveys are formed primarily for protection from predators and for warmth during the winter. When the nesting season comes, the coveys break up. Birds without mates may stay together in smaller groups.

Quail, like some penguins, retain the same mate every year if it is possible. They build their nests on the ground, in well-concealed spots. The females generally incubate the eggs, while the males guard the nest. When the chicks are hatched, both parents share in their care and feeding. Sometimes a mother will lay a second clutch of eggs soon after the first has hatched. She incubates them while the father raises the first group. That is called double brooding. Double brooding is one way quails increase their reproductive potential.

The reproductive potential of an animal is the number of offspring a pair could produce under perfect conditions. The number varies widely from animal to animal and species to species, and it depends on many factors. With quail it depends on such things as how many eggs are laid in a clutch, how often clutches are laid, how many years the parents are able to produce eggs, and the percentage of eggs that actually hatch. Since predators, disease, bad weather, food shortages, and the like always claim the lives of some offspring — or prevent the parents from producing them at all — reproductive potential is always higher than the actual number of surviving offspring. It is, therefore, an advantage for animals like the quail to have a large reproductive potential to help make sure sufficient numbers survive to continue the species.

R
Rose

Roses, in some form, have been in existence for at least 30 million years. They are members of the family Rosaceae, which includes such fruits as apples, cherries, peaches, pears, strawberries, and raspberries. Roses grow in almost every part of the world, from the Arctic Circle to equatorial jungle, in both wild and cultivated forms.

pear   *apple*   *peach*   *crab apple*

The first known references to roses are found in the writings and art of the ancient Sumerians, in what is now Iraq. The first references to cultivated roses are from China, in the writings of Confucius. These references place the gardening of roses at least 2,500 years ago.

From left: Chinese, Medieval, Indian, and Italian designs using rose motifs

Both the Greeks and the Romans were fond of the flower and used the petals and extracted oil in ceremonies and celebrations. Roses have a special significance in the Christian religion, symbolizing purity, health, and virtue and having associations with the Virgin Mary. Roses have been described and honored countless times by poets, novelists, playwrights, artists, and musicians. They richly deserve the title "Queen of Flowers."

There are about two hundred kinds of wild, or "species," roses. They often have open, cup-shaped flowers with from five to twelve petals. They are not what comes to mind when we think of a "typical" rose. The blossoms of species roses vary in size from a tiny ½ inch wide to 4 inches wide. The bushes may grow as high as 30 feet.

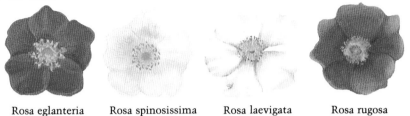

Rosa eglanteria   Rosa spinosissima   Rosa laevigata   Rosa rugosa

Cultivated varieties, or "cultivars," are the roses we see, grow, and buy most frequently. They are not true species but varieties that have been created by crossing two different parent flowers. There are literally thousands of rose cultivars, in a multitude of colors, shapes, sizes, scents, and plant types. Here are just a few:

Sea Foam   Poker Chip   Sea Pearl   Summer Sunshine   Crested Moss   Precious Platinum

Montezuma   Sundowner   Camareux   Persian Princess   Handel   Cricket

The process of crossing different flowers to create new cultivars is called hybridization. It is used to produce plants and flowers with a combination of desirable characteristics inherited from the parent plants. It is not unlike what dog breeders do to develop new breeds, which are all members of the species *Canis familiaris*. Rose cultivars may be crossed for shape, size, or scent of the flower, hardiness in cold weather, resistance to disease and pests, and length and frequency of flowering.

Hybridization has for many years been used to create hardier and more productive strains of food crops, such as corn and rice, as well as to create new varieties of decorative flowers. Recent advances in genetics, which is the study of the mechanism of inheritance, have allowed great gains in this field and promise many more.

S

Snail

The mollusks are a large and important animal group, second only to the arthropods (insects, spiders, and mites) in number of species. Snails, along with octopuses, squids, clams, and others, are members of Mollusca. The snails are by far the largest and most widespread group of mollusks, with some 40,000 species on land and in the sea.

Snails are referred to as gastropods, meaning "stomach foot," which refers to their distinctive means of locomotion. Like most mollusks, they are protected by a hard shell. Twenty-four thousand of the snail species are land dwellers and are the only mollusks to have left the sea. That probably occurred at about the same time the first plants moved to land, around 350 million years ago.

lesser zonite snail

banded Florida tree snail

elegant little helix

Van Nostrand's forest snail

Land snails can be found in a variety of habitats, but most frequently in forest or jungle, preferring moist, shady areas. Many smaller species are found in the top layers of soil, where they feed on decaying plant and animal matter. Others may be found in trees and foliage or near bodies of water. Some snails are so well adapted to life on land that they can survive for years without food or water in a state called estivation, a sort of dry-weather hibernation.

speckled garden snail

white-lipped pupa snail

bent forest snail

heavy forest snail

Land snails do not possess highly developed brains. Their eyes are located at the end of retractable stalks that are often mistaken for antennae or feelers. Locomotion via the snail's single "foot" is made possible by a rippling motion, which proceeds from head to tail. The snail's reputation for slowness is well deserved. An average land snail can chug along at about 4 inches per minute, while a smaller, "speedy" variety can manage a foot or more per minute. Most snails can withdraw into the safety of their shells when they are threatened.

Snails move by means of a rippling motion that proceeds from head to tail.

These shells have always fascinated people. They have been collected and traded, used as jewelry and money, and admired for the variety of their shapes and colors. But why is a snail's shell so often a spiral? The study of the forms and structures of animals and plants, called morphology, provides an answer.

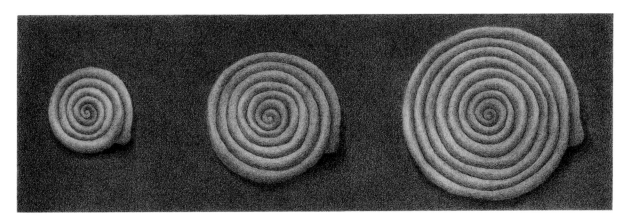

The snail does not discard its shell as its body grows, the way a lobster does, for example. Instead, the shell grows — or rather, is added to — in order to accommodate the growing snail. The older, smaller sections near the center of the spiral are no longer used. By simply adding to what is already there, the snail maintains a roomy home without periodically having to create an entirely new one. The spiral shape is an efficient way for the shell to grow, using the least amount of new material to achieve the result.

T

Tern

The forty-two species of terns are members of the family Laridae and are closely related to the sea gulls. Terns are highly aerial birds and are well adapted for life on the wing, where they spend more time than most other birds do. Terns are relatively small and light, with a streamlined shape, long, pointed wings, and a deeply forked tail. The latter has earned them the nickname "sea swallow," although they are not related to the swallow. Terns have legs that are short and not very useful for swimming or walking. Feeding is done in flight, with shallow dives to capture small fish and crustaceans.

fairy tern

royal tern

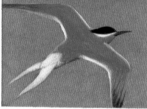
arctic tern

common tern

Terns are coastal ocean dwellers. They breed on small rocky islands, isolated from most predators, and may also roost on sand bars or floating objects. They are highly social birds, feeding, resting, and breeding in small groups or large colonies. Like penguins, the tern parents share the job of incubating eggs and feeding the young. Most terns can be found year round in warm-water areas, but several species are migratory.

The most amazing of the migratory terns is the Arctic tern, a handsome bird that closely resembles the common tern. The Arctic tern has summer breeding grounds in the far northern hemisphere, frequently north of the Arctic Circle. When winter arrives there, the bird migrates to the extreme *southern* hemisphere, where it is summer at that time. Many terns take up residence on the massive ice packs around the coast of Antarctica. The round trip, from Arctic to Antarctic and back, can be as long as 22,000 miles.

From left: The monarch butterfly, Canada goose, and caribou are all migratory animals.

Migration is the regular movement by a species of animals between areas inhabited during different seasons of the year. Nearly every animal group in the world has some member species that migrate. In some cases huge distances and tremendous endurance are involved. Migratory birds are well equipped for their journeys, though it is not known precisely how they find their way from place to place.

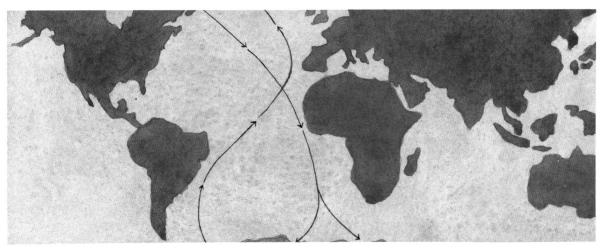

One of several routes used by arctic terns on their long migration

Young migratory birds are born with a general directional sense that in some species enables juveniles that have never migrated to find their wintering grounds entirely on their own. Their accuracy, though, is much better when they are accompanied by adults that have gone before. In addition to the innate (inborn) sense, migratory birds, such as the Arctic tern, may take advantage of visual landmarks, the position of the sun and stars, tastes and smells peculiar to specific areas, and even the magnetic fields of the earth to guide them on their long trips.

In the distant past, migration was probably a necessity brought on by seasonal changes in climate. Now it is an inherited, internally controlled pattern of life for migratory birds.

41

U

Ungulates

The term *ungulate* refers to a large group of mammals with a particular physical attribute in common, that of hoofed feet. Ungulates come in every imaginable shape and size, from the tiny mouse deer to the tall, elegant giraffe to the tapir, the latter little changed for millions of years. Many ungulates have been domesticated and play important roles in our lives. Horses, cattle, sheep, and pigs are just a few examples.

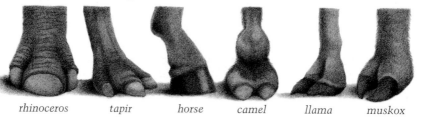

rhinoceros   *tapir*   *horse*   *camel*   *llama*   *muskox*

Ungulates can be divided into two distinct groups—the order Perissodactyla, or odd-toed ungulates, and the order Artiodactyla, or even-toed ungulates. The two groups are classified on the basis of a physical *difference* rather than a similarity: the actual structure of the hoof.

Indian rhinoceros   *Asiatic tapir*   *plains zebra*

The perissodactyls bear their weight primarily on a central digit, the longest toe on each foot. This order includes the family Equidae (horses, zebras, and wild asses), the family Rhinocerotidae (rhinos), and the family Tapiridae (tapirs). All mammals are descended from five-toed ancestors, but in the horse family only the central toe (or digit) remains, encased by the hard hoof (see *E*). The rhinos and tapirs have three digits per foot (four on the tapirs' fore feet) and bear most of their weight on the middle toes. All toes on these two animals are individually hoofed.

The artiodactyls are a much larger and more varied group. They bear their weight primarily on *two* central digits, with two additional digits to the sides in some cases. The order Artiodactyla includes the family Bovidae (antelope, cattle, bison, buffalo, goats, and sheep), the family Camelidae (camels, llamas, vicuñas, guanacos, and alpacas), the family Giraffidae (giraffes and okapis), the family Cervidae (deer), the family Antilocapridae (pronghorns), the family Hippopotamidae (hippos), the family Suidae (pigs), the family Tayassuidae (peccaries), and the family Tragulidae (chevrotains, or mouse deer).

bison   alpaca   okapi   mule deer

pronghorn   hippopotamus   warthog   peccary   chevrotain

The scientific names for the orders and families just listed are part of a system of classification that includes all living creatures on the earth. The system is generally called the Linnaean system, after the Swedish botanist who formalized and greatly expanded it in the 1750s. The system consists of broad "higher" categories, starting with kingdoms, which are then divided into more and more specific subcategories according to the similarities and differences of the organisms — that is, their relationship to one another.

Carl von Linné

1. KINGDOM	4. ORDER
2. PHYLUM	5. FAMILY
3. CLASS	6. GENUS
	7. SPECIES

All names are either Latin or Latinized words, and the genus and species names together make up each organism's scientific name. For example, *Ceratotherium simum* is the white rhinoceros. It belongs to the kingdom Animalia, the phylum Chordata, the class Mammalia, the order Perissodactyla, the family Rhinocerotidae, the genus *Ceratotherium*, and the species *simum*. The scientific name is always in italics. The first letter in the genus name is always capitalized, and the species name is lowercased.

V

Viceroy

The viceroy is one of the 20,000 or so species of butterflies in the world. As a member of the order Insecta, it has three body segments, six jointed legs, an exoskeleton, and a pair of antennae. The adults have, as all butterflies do, two pairs of wings and a coiled-up "nose" for drinking nectar from flowers. They also grow like all butterflies, starting as eggs, hatching as caterpillars, lying dormant as pupae, and emerging fully metamorphosed as butterflies.

Hypolimnus dexithea

American marsh fritillary

Catacore kolyma

tiger swallowtail

red lacewing

It is the wings and the colorful patterns on them that have made butterflies an object of special admiration. Venation, the system of veins in the wings, gives them form and strength, while tiny "scales," arranged in overlapping rows, like roof shingles, create the colored pattern.

Viceroys are found throughout eastern North America (south of Hudson Bay), in much of central North America, and in parts of the West. Their wings are deep orange with well-defined black venation and white spots around the edges. The body is also black.

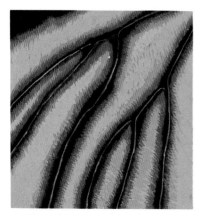
Venation on a viceroy's wing

viceroy

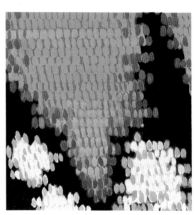
Wing "scales" on a viceroy

Viceroys are successful mimics at every stage of their lives. Their eggs, which they lay on the leaves of willow trees, resemble certain inedible growths often found there. The caterpillars are rather grotesque and slightly ferocious looking and have a blotchy coloration that makes them resemble bird droppings. The vulnerable pupae have similar markings. At both stages, predators may be less than interested in eating the viceroy.

Adult viceroys closely resemble monarch butterflies. Monarchs have an unpleasant taste that predators, primarily birds, quickly learn to avoid (see *L*), and although the viceroys are only mildly unpalatable, they, too, are largely avoided.

viceroy pupa

viceroy caterpillar

In addition to imitating other species, as the viceroy does, mimics may imitate such inedible or unappealing objects as the bark of trees, leaves, twigs, and stones. The process by which the mimic species develop is a gradual one. It might begin when members of an animal population develop, through accident or individual variation, features somewhat like those of the "model" species or object. These individuals may, as a result, get a certain amount of protection and will be more likely to survive and reproduce. Those among their offspring that inherit the features or resemble the model even more will again be more likely to survive and reproduce. Over many, many generations the "mimic" species comes to resemble the model more and more closely and gains more protection as it does.

Malaysian praying mantis

East African silk moth caterpillar

The viceroy (left) has thicker venation and duller coloration than the monarch.

In that way the viceroy (the mimic) has come to look very much like the monarch (the model). A keen eye can tell the difference between the two. Most predators, however, cannot, so the viceroy thrives.

W

Wallaby

Wallabies are members of the family Macropodidae, meaning "large foot." The six species of kangaroos and wallaroos are the largest of the macropods. The numerous related smaller species are together called the wallabies. All are members of the order Marsupialia. As such, their young are generally born in an undeveloped state and enter a protective pouch on their mother's abdomen, where they nurse and grow until they are mature enough to come out.

whiptail wallaby   *red-necked wallaby*   *rock wallaby*   *New Guinean forest wallaby*   *swamp wallaby*

Adult wallabies have the characteristic well-developed hindquarters and large back feet that allow them to hop with agility and speed. The strong tail provides balance in jumping and acts as a sort of third leg when the wallaby is sitting. Running away is the wallaby's best defense, but larger species can deliver a nasty kick when they are threatened.

Whiptail wallabies on the move. Whiptails are among the most social of the wallabies.

Wallabies can be found in a variety of habitats in their native Australia, Tasmania, and New Guinea, including desert, grassland, and forest. Most prefer dense foliage for cover, and most feed during the evening or night on grasses, leaves, and other plants. Many species are solitary, but some, like the whip-tailed and black-striped wallabies, are very social, forming "mobs" of thirty to fifty individuals.

Australia and nearby islands are home not only to the macropods but also to two-thirds of all marsupials and all of the world's monotremes, or egg-laying mammals. Animals of this area in general are a source of fascination to scientists and laymen alike because they are so unlike any others. There is a good reason why.

The echidna (left) and the platypus (right) are monotreme species.

More than 160 million years ago, Australia was part of a supercontinent called Gondwanaland by geologists, which included what are now Antarctica, South America, Africa, New Zealand, and India. This supercontinent gradually broke apart, and the continents inched toward their present positions. For about 40 million years, Australia has been moving eastward across the Indian Ocean, isolated from the other continents. This isolation is what allowed unusual fauna such as the wallabies to develop, undisturbed by the introduction of new animals through migration.

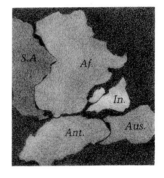

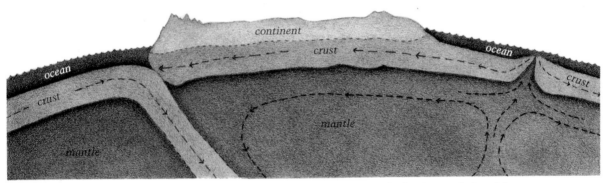

The process of continental movement, or drift, is explained by the theory of plate tectonics. The theory suggests that the earth's rigid outer shell, or lithosphere, is divided into roughly twenty-five "plates." The plates float on a semiliquid portion of the earth's molten mantle, moving outward from "spreading centers," where new material is added to them. The plates come together at "subduction zones," where the edge of one plate dives beneath that of another and back into the mantle. The visible continents are only one portion of these plates. Plate tectonics is important in the study of animal life because it explains how some ancient animals were found on many of the continents as well as how unusual animals like the wallabies came to develop on only a single continent. Although they move much too slowly for us to notice, the continents, and the life on them, are in motion even now.

X
Xylem

Xylem are the special tissues present in vascular plants, that is, those with internal systems for transporting food and water. Xylem are not actual organisms. They are just a part of a living plant, though in some cases the xylem tissues are not even alive when they are being the most useful. They are responsible for conducting water and the minerals dissolved in it to all parts of the plant.

   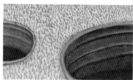

Magnified views of xylem cells that have formed water carrying tubes

It is impossible to overstate the importance of water to plant life. Without water, plants cannot exist. It is not surprising, then, that plants have developed complex ways of collecting, distributing, and storing water.

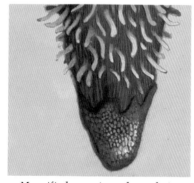 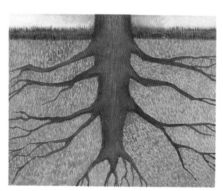 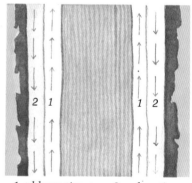

Magnified root tip and root hairs   *Root system of a tree*   *1. phloem tissue   2. xylem tissue*

In most plants, the primary water collector is the root system, in particular the tiny root hairs, which can absorb an amazing amount of moisture from the soil. Water is passed from the roots to the stem, or trunk, where xylem cells known as tracheids conduct the water on its upward path. Those cells are often dead when they are best able to conduct. In some trees tracheids lose some of their cell walls, enabling them to form tubelike vessels that function like water pipes.

The final destination of water is the leaves, where it is used in photosynthesis to create food (see *I*). The food is then distributed around the plant by a separate network made of "phloem" tissues. It is not hard to imagine water traveling to the top of a 3-foot plant, but how does a 300-foot tree move huge quantities of water from its roots to its topmost leaves against the pull of gravity? Two forces allow the tree to do that.

One is the ability of the air around the leaves to absorb moisture. That water loss, called transpiration, exerts a constant pull on the water in the tree, not unlike the effect of sucking on a straw. A second force is the tendency of water molecules to be strongly attracted to one another, especially in such narrow spaces as the xylem vessels. That "cohesion" allows the water to be drawn upward by transpiration in a continuous flow.

venation on a maple leaf

Transpiration pulls large quantities of water upward.

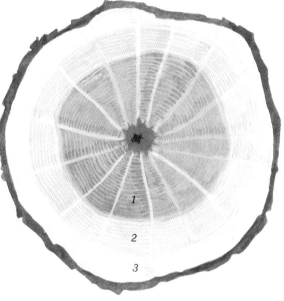

1. heartwood   2. sapwood   3. phloem

Xylem tissue has a second important function, which is to provide plants and trees with strength and rigidity. In nonwoody plants the thick-walled xylem cells provide those qualities best when they are full of water. When they are not, when the plant is overdry, rigidity and strength are lost. The plant wilts. In woody shrubs and trees, xylem tissue eventually loses its water-conducting ability and becomes heartwood, the hardest and most rigid part of the tree. The outer xylem layers, or sapwood, also provide some rigidity but are primarily concerned with maintaining the vital flow of water from root to leaf.

Y

Yak

The yak (*Bos mutus*) is a member of the order Artiodactyla, the even-toed ungulates (see *U*), and the family Bovidae. It is related to the oxen of Southeast Asia, India, and China, including the banteng, the gaur, the seledang, and the kouprey. In its wild form, the yak inhabits a small range at heights of 15,000 to 20,000 feet on the Tibetan plateau. Smaller, domesticated yaks are raised over a much wider area in Asia.

banteng   *gaur*   *kouprey*

The wild male, or bull, yak is a large and impressive mammal, with a strong, massive body and sturdy legs. It may stand 6 feet high at the shoulder and weigh 2,000 pounds or more. Females are about one-third as heavy. Both have long, gracefully curved horns. The coat is short but thickly matted on the top, and very thick and long on the sides, forming a dense protective fringe that reaches nearly to the ground.

wild bull yak

The yak's home range is in the northern Tibetan steppes, the lowlands of which are cold, bleak, and treeless, dotted by marshes and lakes. The highlands are rugged mountains, where sudden, fierce snowstorms can strike, even in the summer, and where few animals venture. Yaks are well adapted to life in both parts of this habitat. Their flat, broad hooves enable them to walk in the marshy lowlands, where they browse on grasses and lichens during the winter. In summer clawlike parts of their hooves enable them to climb with surprising agility in the snowy mountains, out of reach of their only predators, the Tibetan wolf and the human hunter.

Bull yaks are generally solitary but will sometimes travel in groups of three to five. Younger, "bachelor" yaks form groups of a dozen or so, while females and the young band together in groups that can have hundreds of members.

Yaks have adapted, as penguins have (see *P*), to a very difficult environment. The process that allows such adaptations to occur is called natural selection, or, in Darwin's famous phrase, "survival of the fittest."

The muskox (left) and the tahr (right) have also adapted to difficult environments.

In the case of yaks, over the years those animals that have been the healthiest, strongest, and best equipped to survive the cold, harsh steppes have lived and bred and passed on these favorable characteristics to their offspring. Less able or healthy animals survived far less frequently. It should be noted, though, that "fittest" does not necessarily mean "strongest." The millions of species of animals and plants on earth have a multitude of ways of ensuring their chances of survival. Many of them, like the mimicry of the viceroys (see *V*), have little in common with the brute strength and endurance of the yaks.

Z

Zebra Finch

The zebra finch is a member of the weaver finches, a group of small, seed-eating birds that are closely related to the weaverbirds of Africa. The zebra finch is probably the best known of the weaver finches and gets its name from the striking black-and-white pattern of its feathers. Wild members of the species are found in most parts of Australia. The zebra finch is also widely kept as a pet.

parson finch   *Gouldian finch*   *zebra finch*   *double-barred finch*   *masked finch*

This little bird prefers open grasslands with scattered trees and bushes, but it can be found in farmland, pastures, and gardens. The zebra finch is one of the few birds that has managed to live successfully in the desert and semidesert interior of Australia. Long droughts are common there, and rainfall is irregular and unpredictable. The region has no seasonal cycles of wet and dry, as many other deserts have. However, the zebra finch has adapted to this climate very nicely. It drinks much less, as a rule, than other birds do, and can sometimes go for weeks and even months without water.

Because the Australian desert has no weather pattern, the zebra finches have no regular breeding cycle. They nest whenever substantial rains come, and they often start building their nests with the first hints of rain. Females can lay their eggs quickly after the rains begin, in order to take advantage of the plant and insect life that follows and to feed the young.

The nests are spherical and roofed over, woven mostly from dried grasses. They resemble the intricately woven nests of the true weaverbirds but are more loosely constructed. They are built in bushes and low trees. Males and females share in the building of nests and in the incubation of eggs.

Nest building is an extremely important activity for most, but not all, birds. The purpose of the nest is, of course, to provide a safe place to lay the eggs, incubate them, and raise the young. Choice of a nest site is usually made with two things in mind—safety from predators and nearness of food. Bird nests can be found on the ground (see Q), in water, in trees and bushes, in caves and cliffs, and on buildings and other manmade structures. Nest materials vary as widely as their locations and may include mud, grass, stones, twigs, moss, wool, feathers, string, or paper, depending on the habit of each species. Some birds even use sticky cobwebs to bind their nests.

Clockwise from top left: The nests of flamingos, sea gulls, a wood pewee, and baya weavers.

Smaller, more vulnerable birds, such as the zebra finch, tend to build more elaborate and protective nests, spending large amounts of time and energy making sure that their young have a safe, secure home.

Index